ULK™

OFFICIAL FILM ANNUAL

C000285927

£6.99
UK ONLY

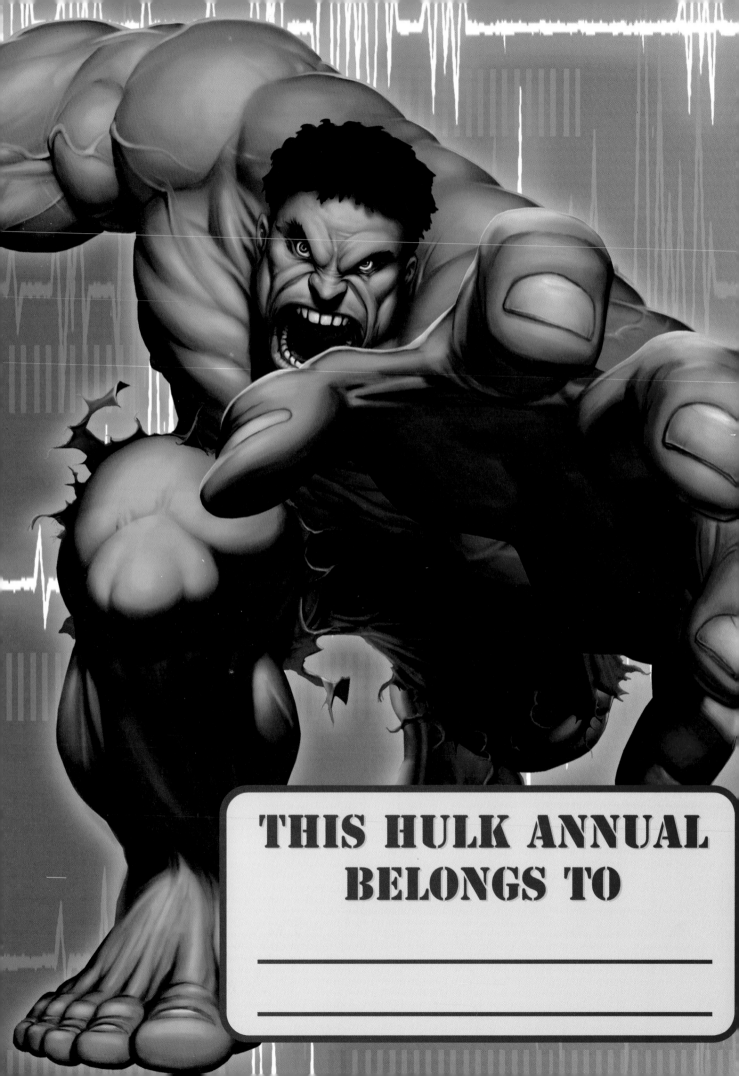

THIS HULK ANNUAL
BELONGS TO

_____

_____

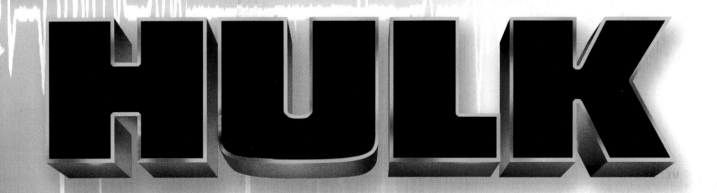

HULK

CONTENTS

Adapted by Jane Clempner
from the novelisation by Peter David
Based on the motion picture screenplay
Story by JAMES SCHAMUS
Screenplay by JOHN TURMAN and MICHAEL FRANCE and JAMES SCHAMUS
Designed by Craig Cameron
Edited by Jane Clempner and Brenda Apsley

THE HULK Movie: © 2003 Universal Studios. Licensed by Universal Studios Licensing LLLP.
THE INCREDIBLE HULK and All Related Comic Book Characters:
TM & © 2003 Marvel Characters Inc. All Rights Reserved.
Published in Great Britain in 2003 by Egmont Books Limited,
239 Kensington High Street, London, W8 6SA.
Printed in Italy
ISBN: 0 7498 5855 9

DAVID BANNER

A quiet, yet desperate genius obsessed with his search for the truth. But his lifetime's research into super-immune systems meets with one stumbling block – General Thaddeus Ross.

Dismissing Banner's theories as dangerous and stupid, the General forbids him from using human subjects. So David Banner takes the only option left – himself.

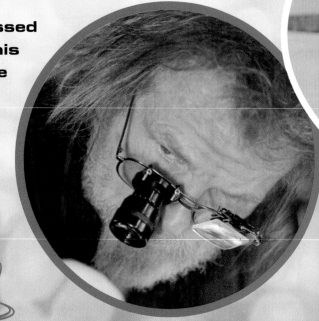

GENERAL THADDEUS 'THUNDERBOLT' ROSS

So-called because of his fierce temper and ability to destroy anyone who crosses him, he's an army man through and through.

Sometimes cold and emotionless, his sense of duty matters more than anything – even his precious daughter, Betty.

When his wife dies and a rift grows between himself and his daughter, the General only has one thing left – his love for his country.

GLEN TALBOT

The handsome, up-and-coming soldier that General Ross would like his daughter to settle down with, Glen Talbot is not all he seems.

An opportunist and power-seeker, he is jilted by Betty and leaves the army to join a large private research organization called Atheon.

Betty has only one thing to say about Glen Talbot. Watch your back!

BETTY ROSS

Brought up by her father, Betty grows into a beautiful young woman, the image of her late mother. As an ace student, and against her father's wishes, Betty decides to become a scientist rather than settle down with a 'nice lieutenant'.

Losing contact with her father, she now works alongside Bruce Banner at the Lawrence Berkeley laboratory.

They fall in love, but she soon finds him incapable of showing his emotions. So, can they become just good friends?

BRUCE BANNER

With an IQ of 187, Bruce is not like other children! Growing up with his adoptive mother – Mrs Krenzler – he learns from an early age to bottle up his feelings. But his world is filled with nightmares. Strange, vivid memories haunt him and he is tormented by voices in his head. Teased and bullied, he struggles to control his emotions – and his anger.

As an awkward teenager he is more interested in science than girls, and decides to become a genetic scientist, like his dead father. As project administrator at the Lawrence Berkeley lab, he is now leading research into human cellular response. His cool head and emotional detachment serve him well, until the day he learns the truth about his past...

PROLOGUE

It was Christmas in the Banner house not far from the army base out in the Nevada Desert. The lights on the artificial tree in the living room sparkled. Three-year-old Bruce played while his dad, David, bounced two little stuffed toys just out of his reach. Young Bruce laughed. Tears rolled down his father's cheeks. He knew this brief moment of happiness could not last.

Wiping away the tears, David Banner went to his study and pulled out a syringe and test tube. He gripped his three-year-old son's arm and stuck the needle in.

"David, what the hell are you doing?" His wife stood in the doorway – she had returned unexpectedly. The syringe fell to the ground, splattering blood.

Little Bruce began to howl and his mother turned white as she watched what was happening to her son. His howling grew louder and the veins on his temples began to bulge. Then his arms started to expand and his body convulsed as bumps and ripples bubbled under his skin. Edith Banner fainted and the heavy thud of her body made young Bruce stop crying.

David Banner seized his chance. Pointing a finger at his son, he snarled, "You did this, Bruce! You hurt your mummy!"

"N-no," stammered the little boy, horrified.

"Yes!" snapped his father. "Because you cried. See what happens when you get upset? Bad things happen. And if you let yourself get upset, more bad things will happen. Do you understand?"

Little Bruce began to sob.

"You're doing it again! Don't do it. Maybe your mummy will die and it will be your fault. Do you hear? Smash the anger. Smash it! Understand?"

Bruce scrambled into bed, terrified. His father clicked off the light, leaving his son in darkness, except for a small, green nightlight. Bruce stared at the green glow and his father's words burned into the depths of his memory.

Things were about to get worse for David Banner. His wife knew too much. And then he was called to General Ross's office.

"We've found samples of human blood in your lab, Banner," said the newly-promoted General. "I gave you strict instructions not to use human subjects for your research. You've ignored my orders, so you're off the project. Shut down what you're working on, and leave the base."

It was all Bruce's fault, thought David Banner. His experiments on himself were going fine until he had a son and passed on the mutagens in his blood. The boy was a monster. It was his blood that had been found in the lab. Did they want it shut down? He'd show them!

The alarm bells around Desert Base began to ring out. The entire base was about to explode...

EVACUATE!

General Ross put little Betty into the back seat of his jeep and hurtled towards the Banner house. He was furious with himself and with Banner. He pulled up outside the house. Betty peered toward the top window where she saw a small boy looking out. She waved. In the distance, the air was split by an earth-shattering explosion, and that was when the screaming began...

Many years later, Desert Base Nevada was rebuilt and memories of the explosion began to fade. But the screaming lived on in the nightmares of those who had seen it happen...

CHAPTER ONE

FROG NUMBER ELEVEN

Bruce Krenzler stepped out of the shower and looked at himself in the mirror. His eyes stared back at him with intensity and hatred. He'd seen the look before. He blinked it away and studied himself. He had straight black hair, ears that stuck out a bit, and a reasonable body - he didn't get time to exercise as he was so busy at the lab. He hurried to get dressed and headed for the Lawrence Berkeley laboratory where he was project administrator. He cycled to work. He was late. His assistant, Jake Harper, had already put Freddie the frog on his pedestal inside the gamma sphere.

Bruce and Harper made their final checks.

"Release the nanomeds," said Bruce. Harper pressed the release valve. There was a hissing sound as the chamber inside the gamma sphere filled with gas. The frog heard the soft hiss of the gas and flicked out his tongue, hopefully.

"Okay," said Bruce, "let's hit Freddie with the gamma radiation." Harper punched instructions into a keyboard and a pinpoint of

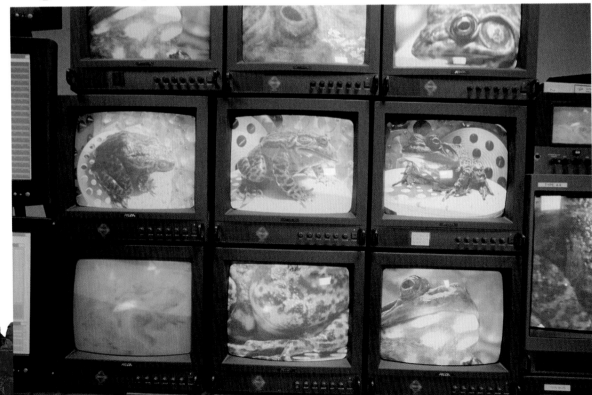

gamma radiation hit the lens above the frog, then zapped the creature across his chest. Freddie flipped over onto his back, then righted himself, revealing an ugly gash on his chest. The frog was disorientated and blinked furiously.

For a moment, nothing happened. Then slowly, miraculously, the wound began to close up, leaving a small zone of throbbing, fluorescent green around it. Bruce couldn't believe it.

"Yes!" said a triumphant voice next to him. He turned to see Betty standing there. Bruce smiled at her, then studied the reading from the scanners under the frog. Freddie the frog trembled slightly. Then he exploded.

Harper let out a tragic cry, as the frog's innards splashed all over the inside of the dome. Bruce didn't let any emotion show on his face. Freddie was just frog number eleven. The other ten had all died much faster. He really thought this one was going to beat the odds. It was another disappointment.

Bruce and Betty chatted as they went to the cafeteria.

"I saw my father in the news," she said. "He got another medal from the President."

"You should call and congratulate him," suggested Bruce.

"The thought had crossed my mind," replied Betty. "And you should think of finding out more about your real parents, who they were, what happened to them."

"Not again," sighed Bruce.

"Don't you want to know more about where you came from? It might do you good – open you up to more feelings."

"And why should I want more feelings?" snapped Bruce.

Betty's reply confused him. "I can wish, can't I?"

Bruce's emotional detachment was more useful when dealing with the Board of Directors. They had called a meeting to hear how the research was progressing. Bruce and Betty had to explain, in simple terms, what their project was about.

"First the nanomeds – little molecular machines – are inhaled into the organism," explained Betty. "Then we awaken them with gamma radiation. Once awakened, they respond to cellular distress – a wound for example – by making copies of healthy cells and breaking down the damaged ones."

Bruce took over. "The main problem is we've yet to find a living body that can survive the force of the cellular activity and the discharge of the waste products created from the damaged cells. If we succeed we may realise the possibility of near-instantaneous bodily repair."

The Board was clearly impressed. Their work was beginning to spark interest

from the medical world and the Army was interested too. It was no surprise then that Betty had a visit from her old flame – Glen Talbot.

Although he had swapped his Army uniform for a crisp business suit he still looked like a soldier. He arrived at the lab claiming to be interested in the applications of their research. Betty hadn't seen him for many years and had no real desire to see him now. He had been the cause of the rift between her and her father.

"Your work here could be very profitable in the real world," he smiled, after greeting Betty like a long-lost friend. "How'd you like to come and work for us at Atheon and get paid ten times what you earn here?"

There was no hesitation in her response. "Glen, two words. The door."

With eerie timing, the door opened, and in walked Bruce.

The three of them stared at each other.

"Bruce Krenzler, this is Glen Talbot, I've mentioned him in the past," said Betty.

Bruce looked him up and down. "Oh yes, the Army clown you dated before you went to college?"

Glen chose to ignore this. "My understanding is

that you and Betty work together. And I have an offer to make you from the company I work for – Atheon."

"I'm sorry, but I'm not too happy about your close ties with the military," snapped Bruce.

"I left the Army. Think about my offer – don't answer now." Then he turned to Betty and handed her his business card. "Can I take you out to dinner tonight – to catch up?"

Betty looked at Bruce and thought she saw a flicker of jealousy in his eyes.

Jealousy was better than nothing. "Pick me up here at six," she smiled back at Glen. "No point dismissing new ideas out of hand, is there, Bruce?"

Bruce shrugged, but as he watched Glen Talbot turn and leave he had the eeriest feeling that something or someone else was rooting around behind his eyeballs, growling in annoyance.

Betty has left a coded message for Bruce. Can you decipher it using the secret code below?

A B C D E F G H I J K L M N O P Q R S T U V W X Y Z

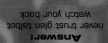

Answer:
never trust glen talbot
watch your back

Bruce is about to press the release switch. Can you figure out which line of gamma radiation leads to Freddie?

A B C D

Answer:
Gamma radiation line C leads to Freddie

WORD SEARCH

The words listed below are all associated with the Lawrence Berkeley laboratory.

Can you find them in the word grid? The words are spelled out forwards, backwards or diagonally.

With a pencil, draw a line through the words you find.

The words to look for are: RADIATION GAS NANOMEDS DOME CATALYST SOLUTION GOGGLES FUNNEL FREDDIE SYRINGE

T	N	A	N	O	M	E	D	S
S	E	G	N	I	R	Y	S	F
Y	D	O	A	X	P	O	R	U
L	G	O	G	G	L	E	S	N
A	A	A	Z	U	D	A	T	N
T	S	A	T	D	L	E	I	E
A	L	I	I	A	A	M	O	L
C	O	E	A	Z	A	O	N	Q
N	O	I	T	A	I	D	A	R

CHAPTER TWO

CHAPTER TWO

THERE'S MONSTERS EVERYWHERE

As the night shadows stretched their fingers across the Lawrence Berkeley laboratory, a lonely janitor pushed his squeaky cart down the main corridor. He kept his face lowered, but when he raised his head to look around, his eyes burned with frightening intensity. Stopping at the door to Bruce Krenzler's office, he went in, passing Betty on her way out.

She paused and looked at him. "Hey, what happened to the old janitor?" she asked.

"Benny's dead. I'm the new guy..."

Bruce was hunched over the paperwork on his desk. Unusually for him, he was letting his mind wander, thinking about Betty going off to have dinner with Glen Talbot. He felt annoyed at himself for letting her go so easily.

He couldn't work, so he stood up and walked into the corridor, his shoes squeaking on the newly mopped floor. Then he heard a whimper. As he turned the corner he saw a small, mangy poodle sitting alone. Bruce walked towards it and reached out to pat it. Suddenly it bared a mouthful

of rotting teeth. "Okay, okay," said Bruce, backing away and leaving the creature growling.

He left the building under a cloudless sky and wondered if the full moon might explain why a Were-poodle was wandering the premises! Then he unlocked his bike and cycled home.

The janitor stepped out from the shadows in Bruce's office. It didn't take him long to find what he was looking for. Running his hand along the top of the chair, he found a hair and held it up to the light. Then he smiled. He didn't do it very often, and it wasn't a pretty sight!

Unaware, Bruce cycled home and worked until the early hours. Now he couldn't sleep. He couldn't even trick himself into sleeping.

the strange poodle from the lab. He had one hand on the phone to call the police. But was it just a man walking his dogs? It was very late. He was tired and his mind was muddled...

He got out of bed and looked outside.

He had the dreadful feeling that someone was watching his house. The wind began blowing the branches of the trees and he could see shapes. Figures. A man, and three dogs. For an instant Bruce thought one might be

The dog-walker moved on until he reached the ramshackle house that used to belong to Benny the janitor. He unlocked the padlock on the gate. The dogs ran in ahead of him and turned to look at him expectantly. He knew his babies well. He reached into his pocket and pulled out chunks of meat to toss to them. They fought with each other over the food – a rottweiler, an alsatian and

a poodle with rotting teeth. He entered the house.

Inside, on one wall was a bed with a sagging, stained mattress. On the opposite wall was a long table stacked with papers. The man tossed them aside to reveal a gleaming, super-thin computer. He sat down and

pressed a button. The light from the screen illuminated his face. On the wall behind the computer was a notice board covered with photos and clippings following Bruce's career. The man reached up and touched one of the photos.

"Bruce," he said, softly. "My Bruce."

He felt in his coat pocket and pulled out a small container. He twisted off the top and, using a pair of tweezers, lifted the hair from the saline solution and placed it on a glass plate and chopped it into pieces with a razor. Then he dropped several pieces of hair into a test tube half-filled with a milky solution and put it into his homemade DNA splitter. The apparatus hummed and he sat staring at his computer, waiting for the result.

Outside the full moon shone and the night was quiet, except for the sound of snarling dogs.

The next morning, after a bad night's sleep, Bruce cycled back to the lab to find Glen and Betty standing together in his office, chatting. His mood was getting worse by the minute.

"What's *he* doing here?" he blurted out, for once not trying to hide how he felt. "I want him to leave. Now."

"Hey, no worries," said Glen, walking towards the door where Bruce was standing. The two men stood face to face, safely out of earshot of Betty.

"I've done my homework," whispered Glen. "The work you're doing here is dynamite. Just imagine it.

Our soldiers on the battlefield could repair themselves instantly. That gives us one heck of an advantage!"

A voice inside Bruce's head began to get louder: Show him who's in charge here.

"That's not the aim of our research," he said, silencing the voice that was urging him to tear Glen Talbot limb from limb.

"You'll be hearing from me," smiled Glen. Then he left and boarded a helicopter for a meeting at Desert Base – with General Ross.

What secret has the janitor confirmed using his homemade DNA splitter? Write out the letters of the alphabet on a piece of paper and number them 1 - 26 to crack the code.

Write the correct answer in the cells below!

Answer:
BRUCE BANNER IS
THE HULK

Bruce feels like he is being watched. Cross out the letters which appear more than once, then rearrange the remaining letters to spell out something, or someone, Bruce should be wary of.

W M K C G D X G
Y A S I O E Y F U R H
B C D X P J T H F N
M P Z Q S U W V L K
B Q E V L Z

☐ ☐ ☐ ☐ ☐ ☐ ☐

There is a fluctuation in the power supply at the Lawrence Berkeley laboratory and the surveillance cameras are on the blink. Can you help the security guard identify these faces? Then unscramble the names and match them to the pictures.

1 UADTSHDE SOSR

2 NLGE BTAOLT

3 VIDDA RNBEAN

4 BCUER NZLEEKRR

5 DEREFDI

6 YTEBT SSRO

A

B

C

D

E

F

Answer: 1-D, 2-F 3-B, 4-A, 5-C, 6-E

CHAPTER THREE

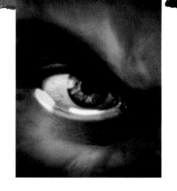

MY NAME IS BANNER

Bruce and Harper began preparing Rick – frog number twelve. But there was a blinking message on the monitor: **Interlock Negative.**

"Hey Harper, is there a problem?" asked Bruce.

"The interlock switch has failed again," said Harper. "I'll go in and see to it."

The interlock switch automatically sealed the sphere when gamma radiation was released. It was vital that it worked. Harper grabbed a safety mask and entered the airlock gamma sphere.

Meanwhile, Betty felt she needed to do something to snap Bruce out of his bad mood. "If it will help, I'll speak to my father," she said. "He can pull a few strings and get Glen off our backs."

"Would you?" said Bruce.

Just then Harper called out through the intercom. "Um, I think the circuit kind of fried. You'd better come and look."

Bruce picked up a mask and went into the experiment area. Just then the interlock switch shorted and cut out. Harper let out a scream, lights began to flash and a recorded voice began the countdown from twenty... to what would be a total disaster...

Harper panicked and tried to back out of the gamma sphere, getting his mask caught so that he

couldn't move his head.

Bruce stayed totally cool and calm. He sprinted into the gamma sphere and pulled the mask free.

Ten, nine, eight...

The interlock door was

Four, three, two...

He hurled Harper out of the gamma sphere.

One, zero. Nanomeds released.

Bruce heard the hissing sound in the gamma sphere.

still open, putting the entire lab facility at risk when the gamma cannon went off. Betty hammered at the keyboard, trying to get the system to shut down.

Seven, six, five...

Bruce looked at Harper, at Betty, at the interlock, at the mask. He dropped the mask.

He had no choice now. He slammed himself against the gamma cannon, blocking the opening, just as the canister released. He heard Betty scream. Then he heard himself scream, then the sound of the interlock, which chose that precise moment to click into place and seal him in.

Now he was howling in pain, but also in satisfaction. At last! He felt as if his face was melting off, and then he fell to the floor, dimly aware of a smile on his face, and he wondered just who was smiling.

In the lab hospital, Betty was expecting the worst. She couldn't believe her eyes when she saw Bruce sitting up in bed, smiling. He didn't smile much, even on his best days!

"He should be the consistency of burnt toast," said the doctor. "But we can't find anything wrong with him!"

Betty stared at him. Then a thought occurred to her. He looked so well, even better than before. Could it be possible that his body had healed itself? Her disbelief turned to excitement and she asked the doctor to leave them.

"You saved my life, Bruce. And Harper's. All of ours," she said.

"Don't be silly," said Bruce. "There was obviously a malfunction. I probably got a dose of nothing more than a fluorescent light – otherwise I wouldn't be here now!"

"No, think about it. The nanomeds hit you first, then the radiation. The nanomeds must have healed you. How else could you have survived?"

Bruce started to laugh. "If that's true... then it worked! We must do the experiment again!"

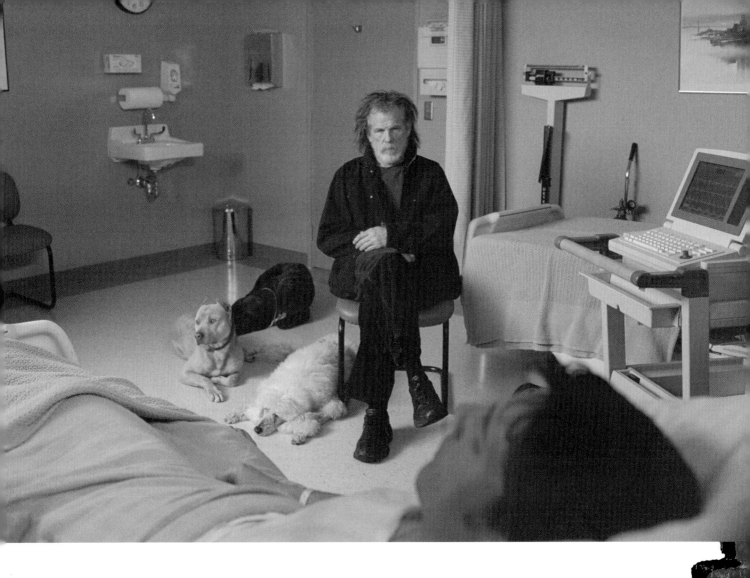

No," said Betty, her scientific brain working overtime. "It's not the experiment – it's you. The radiation, the nanomeds would have killed anyone else. Bruce, there's something different in you."

Bruce scoffed at the idea. But that night, when Betty had gone, he fell into a fitful sleep...

In his dreams, the janitor was at his bedside with his three dogs.

"Your name is Banner, not Krenzler," he said. "You've had an accident and now you're wondering why you're still alive. You're thinking there's something different about you, inside." He shoved his face towards Bruce's, and another image leapt into Bruce's mind.

It was the janitor's face, but much younger. He was shoving some sort of soft toys at Bruce, and laughing.

"Recognise me now?" said the old man. "I am your father."

"No!" cried Bruce. "You're lying. My parents died when I was a child."

"That's what they told you. They put me away. But I'm out now. They couldn't keep me locked up for ever."

"You're crazy! Get out!" yelled Bruce. The dogs were getting fidgety.

"Now, now. We're going to have to watch that temper of yours," laughed the old man, before turning and leaving, followed by his three dogs, their long toe nails click-clacking on the polished floor.

Bruce's nightmare continued through the night, his mind filled with images from the past of all the people who had ever laughed at him, or tried to hurt him. He could see them all, chuckling and sneering, and the world around him was tinted green.

When finally he woke, he stumbled to the bathroom to find that his pyjamas had ripped at the seams. And, looking at his face in the mirror, he could see a green light reflected in his eyes...

As Betty Ross sat down to dinner with her father, Bruce was being released from hospital. He went straight to the lab, desperate to understand what had happened. He began testing his own blood, but the results were always the same: **Insufficient Data.**

He checked and rechecked, late into the night, until his back became stiff and his temples began to throb. He heard the phone ring but answered it too late. It was Betty's mobile number. He tried to call her back but there was no signal. Exhaustion was setting in. It seemed as if things were moving in the shadows.

Then he heard a noise in the corridor - maybe it was that crazy janitor and the dogs. He ran out to see and collided with an equipment cart, sending pain searing through his body. He ran on, hit the wall and bloodied his lip. The world began to spin. He was losing all sense of who he was...

He lifted himself up and an animal cry emerged from within him. The scream echoed around the corridors. His blood thickened and turned green and he felt a strength of fury pounding in his veins, surging through him, releasing all the years of pent up anger... smash, smash, **SMASH!**

The next minute the gamma sphere was being ripped from its housing and tossed through the roof of the lab. Alarms sounded and sirens began to wail.

The monster moved off, knowing he could annihilate anyone or anything that stood in his way.

A security guard looked up as the light of the moon shone through the hole in the roof. "What was that?" he said to an old man who was standing nearby in the shadows.

"A hulking monster," said the old man. "A hulk! That's what it was. Tell everyone a monstrous hulk is out there!"

The security guard ran off to warn others.

The old man chuckled to himself. "I named him once. Who better to name him again?"

The next morning when Betty woke it was as if Berkeley had been hit by a tornado. Driving to the lab she found it surrounded by emergency vehicles and barricades. She could see what appeared to be a gaping hole in the roof.

Horrified, she drove to Bruce's house and found the back door swinging loosely on its hinges, broken. The kitchen looked like a disaster area and she followed the trail of destruction to his bedroom. There she found him sleeping like a baby. "Bruce Krenzler!" she said, with a mixture of relief and surprise.

He sat up in confusion, focused on Betty and said, very slowly, "I'm not Bruce Krenzler. I think my name is Banner."

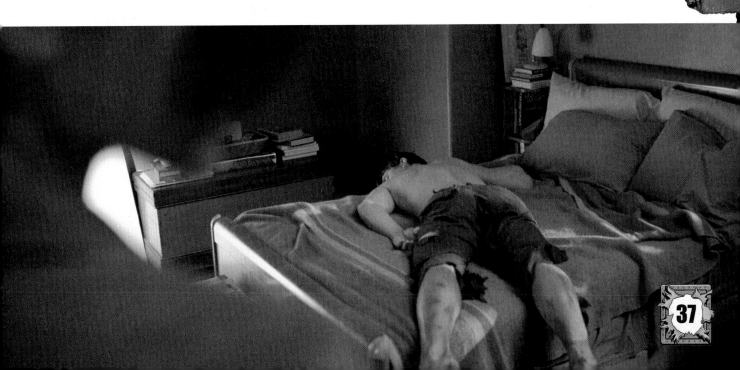

The Hulk smashes anything that stands in his way!
There are ten differences between these two pictures.
Can you find them all?

The following things have changed – Hulk's ear, left arm and shadow are missing. Hulk's eye has changed to red, Hulk's shorts have changed colour to green. The top left skylight is missing, the piece of metal in front of his left foot is missing. On the wall behind Hulk the following things are missing: the lower rail, a crack (top left) and the shadow on the far wall.

Answer:

CHAPTER FOUR

I DON'T THINK YOU'D LIKE ME WHEN I'M ANGRY

Bruce tried to explain what had happened to Betty, but he didn't really know himself. He told her about the janitor and his claims to be his father. He knew something strange was happening to him, something he couldn't control.

"They've shut down the lab and put me under house arrest," he said. "Look outside – the place is surrounded by military police. They obviously think I'm dangerous. You'd better go."

"I'll go when I'm ready," said Betty. "My father has already warned me to stay away from you – but since when did I do as I was told?"

She tried to make light of the situation but, leaving the house, she realized that she was being tailed, too.

Bruce was left alone, a prisoner in his own house. So he was surprised when he heard a mobile ringing. His had been confiscated and his telephone wires cut. Even more surprising, when he answered the phone, he heard his father's voice.

"They want to lock you away like they did me," he began.

"What's wrong with me?" asked Bruce, now desperate to know the truth. "You experimented on yourself, didn't you, and then passed something on to me? And now the gamma rays and radiation have mutated it."

"Released it!" corrected his father. "Now your power is unleashed and I can finally harvest it."

"No way!" said Bruce. "I'll kill it before it does any harm."

"Then you'll have to kill yourself."

Bruce wasn't sure. "I'm a scientist. I know that anything that is done, can be undone. I'll find a way to stop it."

"We'll see," laughed his father. "Meanwhile, I've managed to culture some of your DNA, Bruce, from a single hair. The results are amazing... if a little unstable! I'm sending a sample to your friend Betty... the four-legged kind."

"No! You're crazy," shouted Bruce.

His father hung up.

Bruce ran to the door. Glen Talbot was standing there with a broad smile on his face.

"Inside, you pathetic freak. You're going nowhere!" He shoved Bruce back inside.

"It's Betty, she's in danger."

"I think you're the one in danger right now," said Glen, and with a swift move he kicked Bruce's legs out from under him and pressed a shoe in his face. "Tomorrow you'll be carted off to solitary. But first tell me what happened in your lab."

Bruce's mouth was being crushed under Glen's heel. "You're making me angry," he seethed.

Glen laughed. "Oh, really?"

"I don't think you'd like me when I'm angry."

Glen allowed him to stagger to his feet and then drove a punch into his belly. Only it didn't land. Instead it hit a huge, expanding mass of green

evolutionary ladder. It still looked like Bruce, but distorted and snarling with rage. His cries of pain and release turned to a deafening roar.

Glen staggered back and fell onto the couch. He

flesh. It was growing before his eyes, sweating, ripping clothes, like a volcano exploding. Glen whimpered like a child. He never dreamed of anything so fearsome, and here it was happening before his very eyes.

Bruce's face was widening and flattening out, like a man racing up an

had heard the ridiculous rumours from the people at the lab. But it was no exaggeration. Here was the Hulk!

The Hulk kicked the couch and sent it and Glen crashing through the front window and out onto the lawn. Then he walked through the front wall,

uttering a simple phrase: "Betty, out!"

The soldiers, acting on instinct, started firing, and the bullets bounced off his green hide like little pellets. He took one stride and tossed the soldiers away with a swing of his arms.

Then he was off, making the ground beneath his feet rumble like an approaching earthquake...

Unsuspecting, Betty had managed to lose the guards on her tail, and driven up to the cabin where she used to go for holidays as a child. She wanted to get away to think about everything. She lit a fire and fell asleep in front of it.

She was woken by a noise outside the door. A rustling sound, like an animal. A bear perhaps. She felt afraid and grabbed a torch. She headed out towards the car. Now she realized everything was eerily quiet. Too quiet for the forest.

Half way to the car she stopped and shone the torch around. Huge trees circled the cabin and everything was deathly still. Then she saw something.

"What the..." she murmured. There were two

giant redwood trees with something else between them, something as massive as the trees, and it was green, and it was breathing!

She wanted to run for the car, but her feet wouldn't move. She shone her torch into the eyes of the creature, then she screamed, dropped the torch and stumbled. In a flash the monster was on her, but all it did was hold her in the palm of one hand. She couldn't move. The monster was holding her, staring into her face. She knew that it could have crushed her, but instead it gently lifted her to her car. Unbelievably, the worst was yet to come.

Betty saw them before the creature did. The blood drained from her face as three monstrous dogs, with eyes blazing and saliva dripping from their jaws, emerged from the forest. And attacked.

In rhythm with each other, they bounded,

covering twenty feet with every jump. Betty's protector got her inside the car and faced the dogs, greeting them with a full-throated roar. Then he crouched, leapt, and was suddenly airborne. The dogs tried to follow, jumping up and falling back to earth. They circled in confusion, then stopped, noticing the car. Their thick lips pulled back from their rotting teeth as they started to advance. Suddenly, from overhead, the Hulk descended from his giant leap and landed on the back of one of the dogs. Betty watched in horror as the crushed dog's flesh began to steam and melt away.

The remaining two dogs fought with the Hulk, one dog clamping on to his ankles, the other going for his throat. The Hulk staggered, shook the dog loose from his leg and prized

open the other dog's jaws. Green blood began oozing from his wounds. He leapt up onto the roof of the cabin, leaving the dogs to circle the car. Then suddenly one dog's face was smashed flat against the windshield. The Hulk had uprooted a redwood tree and was using it as a weapon.

The final dog attacked, locking the Hulk in battle. There was a confusion of howls and snarls, biting, mauling and choking, until the Hulk managed to grab the dog's throat and squeeze.

The Hulk staggered down to the river, then stopped and stared at his own reflection in the water. And as he stared, the green skin began to dissolve away into normal flesh.

Betty watched as the Hulk sank down to his knees on the riverbank and witnessed his transformation.

Now there was no denying the truth. Bruce staggered back towards her and they cradled each other, clutching one another like anchors in a world that had turned into a sea of delirious madness.

The following morning the forest seemed strangely normal. Betty and Bruce sat quietly drinking coffee.

"You know what scares me the most?" said Bruce, opening up to her more than he had ever done before. "When it comes over me, when I lose control, I actually like it."

Betty had no idea how to react. "But can you control it?" she asked, nervously.

"I – I don't know. It's just the rage. It takes over."

And that was when Betty decided to call her father...

Help the Hulk through the maze of molecules to become Bruce Banner again.

ODD ONE OUT

Which test tube is the odd one out?

Answer: Test tube 5 is the odd one out.

What emotion makes Bruce Banner change into the Hulk? Choose four letters to spell the word.

X
S
G
Q
N
K
A
P
E
R
H
V
W
J
L
A
O

Answer: RAGE

CHAPTER FIVE

SMASH... SMASH... KILL!

They took him by surprise, with a quick-acting drug in a single dart. Betty felt torn. She had done what she believed to be for the best.

The soldiers picked up the unconscious Bruce Banner and he was helicoptered to a secret underground location.

Now General Ross wanted to find David Banner, but he wasn't an easy man to find. While soldiers were searching his house, he was back at his son's lab. He wanted to be like his son, to feel his power. So he had rigged up the battered gamma sphere and now stood in the chamber, as if awaiting the fate he had always dreamed of. Everything in his life led to this moment. All his work, his lifetime's research.

He spread his arms wide as the radiation bathed his body and the gas-filled nanomeds filtered in. He would make himself more powerful than anyone!

The gamma sphere shut

down and he sagged to his knees. Had it worked? He didn't feel any different. He grabbed the edge of a metal table to help him stand, and cut his flesh. But when he looked down the wound began to mend and glowed silver, like the table! Amazing! He laughed loudly in delight. He had absorbed the properties of the metal. Thoughts raced through his mind. He hadn't expected this!

Bruce was being held under tight security. Glen Talbot walked into his cell with an electric probe. He was battered and bruised from their last encounter.

"What do you want?" asked Bruce.

"I need you to get a little green for me," said Glen, "so that I can take a little piece of the real you, analyse it, patent it and make my fortune. Do you mind?"

Bruce admired his direct approach. "Who are you really working for?" he asked.

"I've told you. A private research organization called Atheon."

"Come on, Atheon

is just a front for something far bigger – some secret branch of the government maybe?"

"Maybe," grinned Glen. "I'll tell you about it sometime. Right now, let's bring the big boys out to play, shall we?" And with that he took the probe and smashed it against Bruce's stomach.

The electric shock sent him flying back against the cell wall.

"By the way," added Glen, "sorry to hear that Betty sold you out to her father and left you. She's gone back to Berkeley, you know."

"You're lying," said Bruce.

"Come on, hit me," urged Glen, amazed at Bruce's powers of restraint.

"Never."

Instead it was Glen who was losing his cool. He sent Bruce crumbling to the floor with a mighty right hook to his chin. Then he started kicking his body, crumpled on the floor.

Just then the door opened and in walked General Ross. "Talbot, that's enough! I am going to speak to my superiors..." They left. Bruce was out cold.

While General Ross was 'speaking to his superiors',

Bruce was being moved to a secure containment tank. There he was wired up to machines for monitoring. With the General out of the way, Glen decided to have some fun.

"Let's shoot some electricity into those brain waves," he grinned.

And in Bruce's brain terrible memories were stirred – of when he was a boy. His real mother was there, only there was a knife, too, dripping with blood, her blood. And holding the knife was his father. And Bruce the boy was screaming and fighting his father. And his father looked into his son's eyes with fear as he saw the monster being released. He sank his teeth into his

father's neck and the screams of the father blended in with the howling sirens. Then there was a terrific explosion outside and the police ran in, and the boy ran to his room and looked out of his bedroom window and saw a car. A little girl in the back seat looked up and waved. And the screaming didn't stop...

Bruce's nightmare turned into a roar. Seams buckled and broke, fluid broke out of the tank, rivets popped, metal twisted and broke, liquid cascaded from the tank as the Hulk rose, dripping and bellowing.

"Smash... SMASH... KILL!"

People ran for their lives as the Hulk smashed his way out of the tank and into the corridor. Glen ordered soldiers to bombard him with gas and foam. Nothing had any effect.

Then General Ross took control. "All units. Spearpoint section Zulu, level 4. Subject is Bruce Banner. All units respond. Secure and neutralize."

"But General, we don't want him dead," argued Glen. "He's no good to me... us... dead."

"My only concern is for the safety of the citizens of this country," said the General. "What's yours?"

Ordering a few men to follow him, Glen grabbed a

laser drill and the most powerful gun he could find and ran after the Hulk. He was the key to his fortune – and he wasn't getting away. They found the Hulk trapped in a corridor of rapidly hardening foam. Glen saw his chance and punched the drill into his neck. He just wanted to get a sample of him. The Hulk recoiled, screaming. His renewed anger gave him the strength to pull free from the foam.

"Retreat!" ordered Glen. He didn't have to say it twice. The Hulk thundered after them,

shaking the walls with each footstep.

Even as he fled, Glen was formulating a plan. If he couldn't get samples of the living monster, maybe he could still be useful dead. He looked at his gun. He could still make his fortune.

Glen turned and stood his ground. Monster and man eyed each other and in that split second the Hulk recognised him and began to grow even more, fed by his anger. Glen could only watch in awe as the green monster

grew to fill the entire corridor and flexed his muscles until the walls started to creak.

"So long, big boy!" said Glen, and unleashed a hail of automatic fire. The bullets bounced off the Hulk and ricocheted around the walls, then back at the man who had fired them. Glen crumbled to the ground, dead.

General Ross saw it all on the security cameras. Glen Talbot had died consumed with greed and corrupted by power. Case closed.

The General had more urgent matters at hand. It

was obvious that ordinary weapons were no good against this monster. He called off his troops. It was time to inform the President.

INTERMISSION

The Hulk is the product of a chain reaction. Can you fit these names into this molecular chain?

BRUCE
DAVID
THUNDERBOLT
BETTY
FREDDIE
GLEN

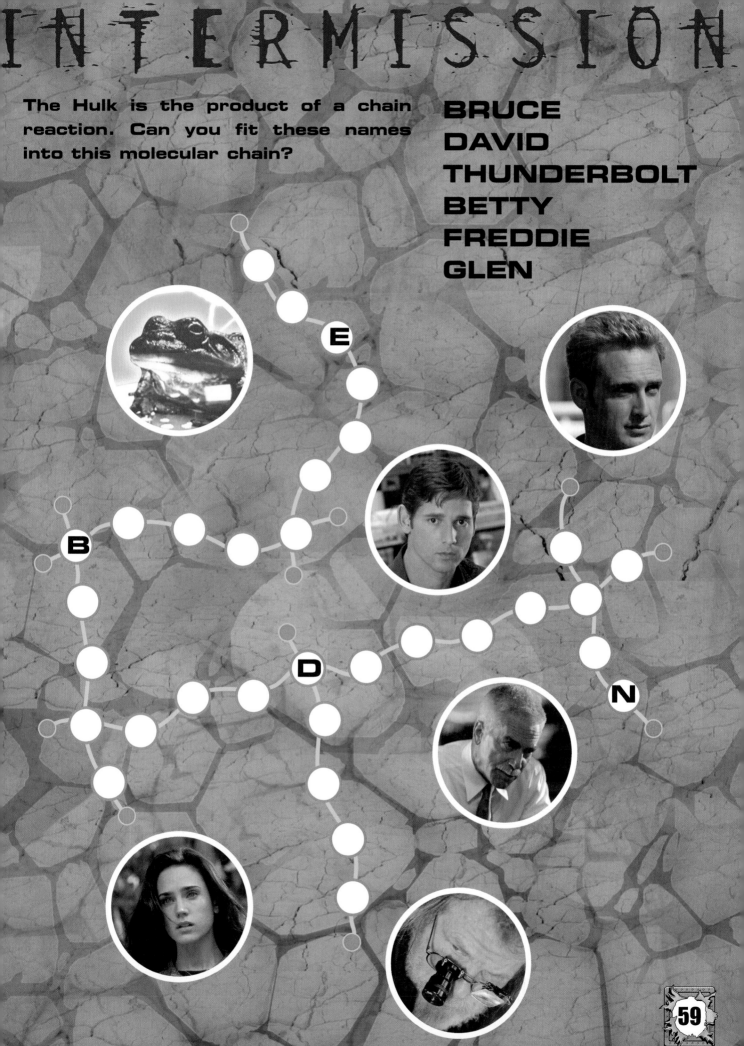

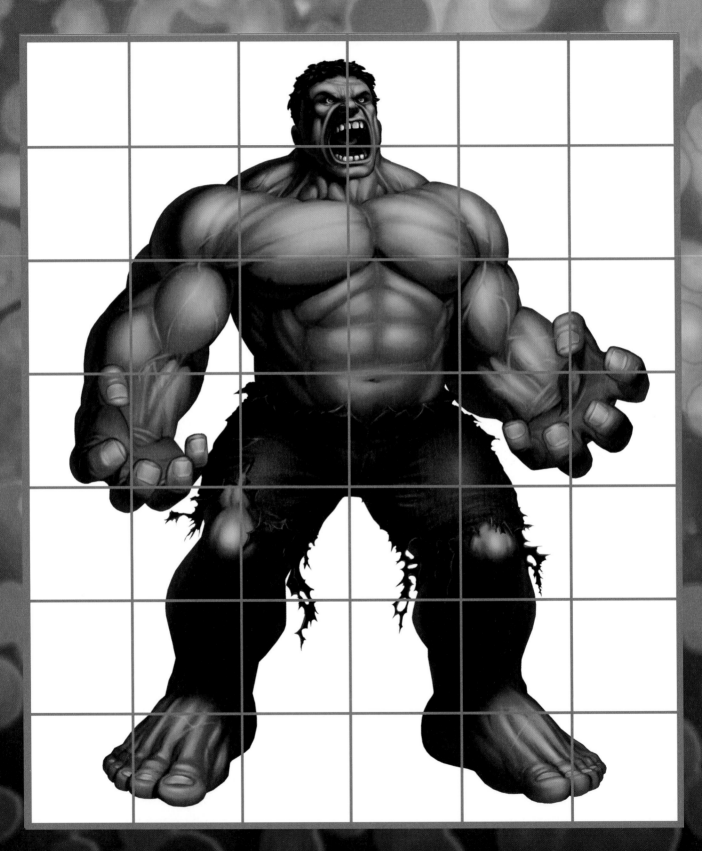

Copy this picture of Hulk square by square,
then use crayons, pens or paint to finish your creation!

CHAPTER SIX

NOTHING CAN STOP ME NOW...

General Ross informed the President and requested more power.

The Hulk tore off through the desert, heading for San Francisco. He dismissed the first wave of tanks like toys. The Blackhawk helicopters couldn't keep up with him. He reached the top of a rocky cliff as the Comanche choppers arrived. He reached out and grabbed the propellers and smashed them against the ground. Their missiles didn't even scratch him. He charged on...

Meanwhile, Betty had been escorted home and found David Banner waiting in her house. He explained everything to her and begged her to speak to her father. He promised to give himself

up if he could just see his son for one last time.

So she brought him to the base and he was locked in a cell, waiting for his moment to come.

The Hulk arrived on the Golden Gate Bridge with a leap. But now three Raptor F-22 jets were after him. Timing his jump perfectly, he leapt up towards one of the jets and landed on top. He clung on as it rose up through the clouds. Frost began to cover him. He lost consciousness and slid off, tumbling and crashing into San Francisco Bay, sending up a geyser of water that could be seen for miles. His body sank to the bottom and lodged in the mud.

Ross felt triumphant, but only for a moment. The Hulk re-emerged from the water and more Blackhawks opened fire. Bullets splattered the water and the Hulk took a deep breath and went under again.

Now Ross was afraid. He felt sure the Hulk could hold his breath for a long time. And there were sewers leading directly from the bay into the heart of the city...

Nobody noticed the first small crack in the street. Then the other cracks came. People noticed now and began to jump out of the way. "Earthquake!" they screamed. The cracks grew. Water mains began to break. Cars careered into each other. Then everyone froze as the head of the Hulk appeared from beneath the street. He let out a roar and panic set in.

The police and soldiers couldn't get through the flood of fleeing pedestrians. Helicopters began to arrive and SWAT teams took up positions on overlooking buildings. The Hulk stood in the middle of it all, and roared.

Then General Ross's voice was heard on a loudspeaker. "All units, hold your fire. I repeat. Do not fire."

Betty walked from the crowd and approached the Hulk. When he saw her, to everyone's surprise, the monster dropped to his knees and let out a cry of pain and shame. She came up to him and touched his face, gently, as if reassuring a terrified child. And, slowly, the Hulk's body began to

contract. Everyone stared in stunned silence as the massive monster dissolved into a harmless human being.

"You found me," said Bruce.

"You weren't hard to find," she replied.

"I'm glad we got the chance to say goodbye," he said. And they clung to each other, surrounded by the wreckage left by the Hulk.

The General picked Betty up by helicopter. "I have no choice," he said. "I have to destroy him."

"You can't," she pleaded. "If you make him mad again you know what will happen."

He knew she was right.

"Give him some breathing room. Let everything calm down. There must be some other way."

General Ross gave the order and Bruce Banner was airlifted to a nearby prison base while military leaders decided what to do. He was held in a specially built tight-security hangar. If he showed the least sign of 'getting angry' there were two electromagnets aimed at him – he would be incinerated in seconds.

Bruce knew the awful truth. He was too dangerous to live.

Back in his cell, David Banner laughed. His time had come. As promised, he was to be allowed to see his son for one last time.

"Soon," he whispered, "soon I will be invincible."

"I should have killed you," David Banner said, walking towards his son for the last time.

"I wish you had," said Bruce. "I remembered last night what you did. You murdered my mother – I don't even know her name." Bruce began to cry and his father reached out a manacled hand to touch him. Bruce recoiled, but his father grabbed his leg. "You see – I have found a cure – for me!" David Banner began to laugh. "My cells can transform too. I used your gamma sphere and now I absorb energy from anything I touch. I gave you life, now you must give it back to me – only a million times more powerful!"

Bruce tried to pull away, realising his father had some terrible plan, something more evil even than the Hulk. He had to put a stop to it all. So he leapt up and urged the electromagnets to fire. They began to power up, but his father grabbed one of the wires and ripped it apart. Then he held the live wires in his hands, just as the soldier at the controls pressed down on the switch. The electromagnetic energy surged straight into David Banner, who cackled and broke open his handcuffs. He

flung out his arms, sending out an electromagnetic field that made the entire hangar sizzle.

David Banner looked over at where Bruce had been thrown by the force and was met by a huge green fist, which lifted him into the air, through the roof of the hangar and threw him across the bay. The Hulk, with a roar, leapt after him.

But now David Banner stood almost as tall as the Hulk. "Nothing can stop me now, I absorb it all and give it back!"

The Hulk attacked, but with each blow David Banner got bigger and greener, absorbing the Hulk's energy and cellular structure. The Hulk stepped back, confused.

"Go on, son. The more you fight me, the more of you I become!" roared his father.

Then the Hulk lifted an enormous boulder and

crashed it down on his father, turning him into stone. The Hulk battered the stone to a mountain of dust. But in doing so, his father re-absorbed his energy and re-shaped into another version of the Hulk!

The two locked in battle at the edge of the bay. But as David Banner absorbed more energy, so the Hulk weakened. Finally the Hulk seemed to dissolve and his father stood victorious, towering above the mountains.

But now the reactions in his body were spiralling out of control. His body was absorbing everything, always seeking new energy sources. And when there was nothing else left, it started to absorb itself. He clutched his stomach, and screamed. Then he stumbled from the mountain, just as fighter planes approached from behind releasing missiles that blew him apart.

A massive explosion engulfed the sky.

Betty spent all her time at the lab after that. She knew Bruce could not have survived the explosion. But she also knew that her phones were still bugged and her house was under surveillance, so somebody obviously thought he was still alive. If he was, she prayed that he would never try to speak to her, for his own sake.

But in her heart she still loved him, and always would.

 EPILOGUE

In a jungle clearing, three Red Cross workers were helping local families. One of them, a man with a beard and long hair, was handing out medicine to children. He spoke in Spanish.

Suddenly a group of soldiers came out of the bush. They were armed. They pushed the families aside and started rifling through the medicine.

"Hey!" said the Red Cross worker. "These people need those medicines."

"Who are you, foreigner, to tell me what to do?" said the soldier. "I will take these medicines. They are the property of the government now."

The Red Cross worker stood in his way. "Put those back," he said, "and get out of here." He had a pounding in his head.

"What!" laughed the soldier.

"You're making me angry," said the Red Cross worker, then a growl came out of his throat that sounded inhuman, and his eyes snapped open, glowing a deep shade of green.

And these were the last words he spoke before the screaming began: "You wouldn't like me when I'm angry..."

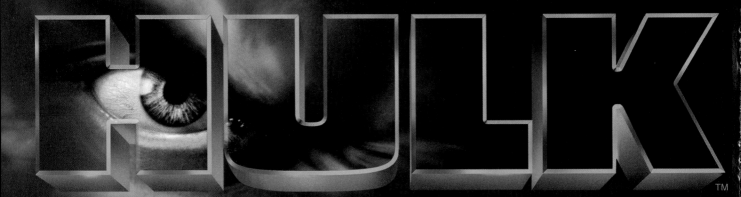

HULK™

The eyes
are the gateway
to the soul...
but whose soul?